MY LiFe
as a
Cowboy
Cowpie

BOOKS BY BILL MYERS

The Incredible Worlds of Wally McDoogle (19 books):

—*My Life As a Smashed Burrito with Extra Hot Sauce*
—*My Life As Alien Monster Bait*
—*My Life As a Broken Bungee Cord*
—*My Life As Crocodile Junk Food*
—*My Life As Dinosaur Dental Floss*
—*My Life As a Torpedo Test Target*
—*My Life As a Human Hockey Puck*
—*My Life As an Afterthought Astronaut*
—*My Life As Reindeer Road Kill*
—*My Life As a Toasted Time Traveler*
—*My Life As Polluted Pond Scum*
—*My Life As a Bigfoot Breath Mint*
—*My Life As a Blundering Ballerina*
—*My Life As a Screaming Skydiver*
—*My Life As a Human Hairball*
—*My Life As a Walrus Whoopee Cushion*
—*My Life As a Mixed-Up Millennium Bug*
—*My Life As a Beat-Up Basketball Backboard*
—*My Life As a Cowboy Cowpie*

Other Children's Series:

McGee and Me! (12 books)

Bloodhounds, Inc. (10 books)

Teen Series
Forbidden Doors (10 books)

Teen Nonfiction
Hot Topics, Tough Questions
Faith Encounter
Just Believe It

Picture Book
Baseball for Breakfast

Adult Fiction
Blood of Heaven
Threshold
Fire of Heaven
Eli

Adult Nonfiction
The Dark Side of Supernatural

www.Billmyers.com

Would you like to interview Bill Myers in your classroom?
See last page for details . . .

the incredible worlds of **Wally McDoogle**

MY LiFe
as a
Cowboy
Cowpie

BILL MYERS

Tommy
NELSON

Thomas Nelson, Inc.
Nashville

MY LIFE AS A COWBOY COWPIE

Published in Nashville, Tennessee, by Tommy Nelson®, a division of Thomas Nelson, Inc.

Unless otherwise indicated, Scripture quotations are from the *International Children's Bible®, New Century Version®*, copyright © 1983, 1986, 1988.

Scripture taken from the *Holy Bible, New International Version* is marked (NIV). Copyright © 1973, 1978, 1984 by the International Bible Society. Used by permission of Zondervan Bible Publishers.

Library of Congress Cataloging-in-Publication Data

Myers, Bill, 1953—
      My life as a cowboy cowpie / by Bill Myers.
      p. cm. — (The incredible worlds of Wally McDoogle ; #19)
      Summary: When Wally and his two best friends spend the summer at a dude ranch, he discovers that writing superhero stories will not help him deal with the cantankerous ranch owner, a deceitful camper, and a dangerous bull named Satan Breath.
      ISBN 0-8499-5990-X
      [1. Dude ranches—Fiction. 2. Ranch life—West (U.S)—Fiction. 3. West (U.S.)—Fiction. 4. Interpersonal relations—Fiction. 5. Christian life—Fiction. 6. Humorous stories.] I. Title.

PZ7.M98234 Myed 2001
[Fic]—dc21   00-054628

Printed in the United States of America
01 02 03 04 05 PHX 06 05 04 03 02 01

For Angela Hunt:

One terrific writer!

"Do not repay anyone evil for evil."

—Romans 12:17 (NIV)

Contents

Chapter 1

Just for Starters . . .

"McDoogle! WHAT ARE YOU DOING, McDOOGLE!?"

Yes sir, I was busy making one of my famous first impressions. This time, it was inside a corral of a tiny little dude ranch. We were all saddling up our horses . . . well, everybody else was saddling up their horses. I was busy just trying to haul my saddle from the tack room over to my horse—not an easy job when you consider the saddle's great weight (and my great wimpiness). It's not that I'm weak; it's just that I've got very specially trained muscles designed only to operate TV remotes and the latest Mario Brothers game.

"Look out!" I shouted, staggering under the saddle. "Coming through!"

"Watch it!" yelled my best friend, Opera.

"You're heading straight for the manure pile,"

1

cried Wall Street, my other best friend (even if she is a girl).

"No problem." I gasped under the weight as I staggered this way and that, then that way and this. "I've got it covered. I know what I'm doing. I'm—

K-SPLAT

smelling kinda bad."

I spotted Cowboy Roy, our beloved counselor, part-time Gestapo, and full-time owner of the ranch, heading toward me. He was about a thousand years old with a brown, leathery face that had more wrinkles than a box of Sun-Maid Raisins. He also had a pretty impressive limp. Thanks to my superkeen insight, I suspected he wasn't exactly thrilled to be having a bunch of kids around his ranch. (My superkeen insight and the fact that all he did was mumble and spit.) Now, as he reached down to pull me out of the pile, he saw no reason to stop.

"Morons," he muttered, then spit on the ground. "I'm surrounded by morons."

"No, sir," I corrected as I grabbed his hand and tried to stand. "I'm not a moron. Just a little unsteady on my feet, that's all. Just a little—

"AUGH . . ." *K-Splat!*
K-SPLAT!

As you no doubt figured, the first "AUGH" and *K-Splat* belonged to me as my feet slipped and I went crashing back into the pile. Unfortunately, the second *K-SPLAT!* was Cowboy Roy, whom I managed to pull down into the pile right along with me.

"MaBOOWLE!!!" (That was supposed to be "McDoogle!" but it was hard for him to speak with his mouth full . . . or for me to hear with my ears full.)

"MaBOOWLE, YOU MOORWON . . ."

Yes sir, I could tell right then and there that it was going to be the start of a beautiful relationship.

An hour later, we were out on the range, herding up some calves to be branded. Well, everybody else was herding up some calves to be branded. I was just sitting on my horse hoping that someday she would move.

You see, Ol' Bag a Bones (who did not get her name by accident) had some problems with me riding her. She hated it. As a result, it had taken longer than usual to establish who was the real boss. But as soon as she made that

clear to me, I did whatever she wanted—even if
it meant letting her stand forever at the edge of
the stream as the calves ran behind us making
their escape.

"McDoogle! Turn your horse around!" Cowboy
Roy cried. "McDoogle, they're getting away!
McDoogle!!"

Now, before we go any further, let me explain
that going to a dude ranch wasn't exactly my
first choice for summer camp. Come to think of
it, it wasn't even my last choice. But Dad, in his
continual quest to make me a man, decided that
riding horses all day would somehow put hair
on my chest. (He didn't say anything about blis-
ters on my rear.) So, when he found the ad in
the paper about this little dude ranch that
worked with only a couple of dozen kids at a
time, he thought, *Perfect . . . another way to
inflict incredible torture upon my son.*

So, there we were—Opera, Wall Street, me,
and about twenty other kids—out in the middle
of the lone prairie, herding bawling calves
through a stream. (Oh, boy. What fun. Maybe
next year Dad will sign me up to be the target
for archery camp.)

"McDoogle! McDOOGLE!"

"Don't worry, sir," a new voice shouted. "I've
got them!"

I turned to see Chad Diamond galloping toward me full tilt, obviously planning to save the day. In a flash, this superrich, superathlete, supereverything of a guy began driving the calves back toward the stream.

"Not bad, kid!" Cowboy Roy shouted. "Nice work!" He turned to the rest of us and yelled, "Why can't you kids handle a horse like that?" He leaned over and spit. "Ya see the way he's workin' him?"

I saw, all right. And I saw something else, too. I saw the way Chad kept stealing looks over at Wall Street. I also saw the way Wall Street kept googling back at him, her face all a-beaming, her heart all a-twittering. I tell you, it was enough to make a guy sick. But before I could break into a major case of nausea, Chad cut his horse behind me and shouted, "Come on, Wally, let's show Cowboy Roy and the kids what we're really made of."

Before I had a chance to point out that that might not be such a good idea, he slapped Ol' Bag a Bones on the rear. No problem, except for the part where it startled her so much that instead of taking off, she raised up on her hind legs and

"Augh . . ."
K-Splash!

threw me into the water.

Now, even that wouldn't have been so bad, if I had taken the time to learn to swim. But with my busy schedule of being Dinosaur Dental Floss, a Toasted Time Traveler, a Walrus Whoopee Cushion, and a Human Hairball, well, it was kinda hard to squeeze swimming lessons into my daily routine.

So, I proceeded to do what any red-blooded kid in my predicament would do . . .

Drown.

Drown and scream my head off:

"Help me! Help me! Help me!"

Fortunately, from all my misadventures, I was a pro at screaming my head off. Unfortunately, there was somebody who was an even greater pro at being a hero. In exactly 2.3 seconds he leaped into the water to rescue me. Normally, I would be grateful for such actions . . . except for three tiny little problems:

Tiny Little Problem 1:
My hero was Chad Diamond.
Tiny Little Problem 2:
When he pulled me up, I discovered I was standing in only three feet of water.

Of course, everybody doubled over with laughter, which was okay by me—except that that brought us to:

Tiny Little Problem 3:
    "Everybody" included Wall Street.

That's right, my good buddy and longtime friend was pointing at me and laughing her head off, just like the rest of the crowd.

Of course, I gave my little idiot smile and pretended to laugh, too. But inside, I was steaming. . . .

* * * * *

"If you ask me, *munch-crunch*," Opera shouted as we peeled off our clothes and limped toward our bunks for the night, "you're just jealous."

"Jealous?" I yelled, moaning and groaning with every step.

"That's, *burp-belch,* right," he shouted.

"No way!" I yelled, whimpering in pain as I crawled up to the top bunk.

Now, in case you're new to these stories (where have you been the last eighteen books?!), let me explain . . .

❏ The *munching* and *crunching* are Opera going through his fifth bag of Chippy Chipper potato chips. Hey, some people have their teddy bears to help them through the night; Opera has his junk food.

❏ The *burping* and *belching* are more frequent features thanks to the case of Pecos Bill's Flame Thrower Hot Sauce recently given to him by the camp's cook.

❏ The yelling was from shouting over the Sony Walkman that Opera had permanently attached to his ears.

❏ And my moaning, groaning, and whimpering? You try riding a horse for six hours and tell me how you feel.

"What do I have to be jealous of?" I called back down to him. "Just because Chad Diamond is superrich and superathletic, why should that bother me?"

"Actually, *crunch-munch,* I wasn't talking about that."

"What then?" I asked.

"You're just steamed because he made you look like a fool when he, *munch-crunch, BURP,* made your horse buck and throw you into the water."

"He what?" I asked. "Are you saying he did that on purpose??"

"Oh, *BELCH,* yeah."

"No way."

But there was no answer.

"Opera? Are you sure? Opera?"

Ditto in the no-answer department. Now all I could hear below me was *munching, crunching.*

"Opera??"

And snoring. Snoring that grew louder by the second.

ZZZZNORK . . . munch, munch, munch
ZZZZNORK . . . crunch, crunch, crunch

That's right, Opera had dozed off. And he'd become such a pro at eating junk food that he was even able to do it in his sleep.

ZZZZNORK . . . munch, crunch,
BELCH!

"Opera?"

But the guy was out cold.

Well, fine! I'm glad somebody could sleep. After what I'd just learned, I sure couldn't. Was it possible? Had super-Chad set me up to look

like a superchump? Not that it would take
much setting up, but still . . .

The longer I lay there staring up at the ceil-
ing, the longer I stewed. Finally, I did what I
always do to unwind. I reached over, grabbed
Ol' Betsy, my laptop computer, and started
another one of my superhero stories. Maybe
that would take my mind off what had happened. Then again, maybe not . . .

It has been another long day of
superheroism for our superhero,
Chester C. Chessclub.

Already he had calculated the pre-
cise location to fire a missile that
blew up some pesky asteroid about to
destroy Earth....Already he had
installed Windows 3001 into every
computer in his school's computer
lab....And to top it off, he even
fixed his glasses with a nice thick
wad of tape around the nosepiece. (Is
there no end to this man's talents?)

Now, at last, he's sitting down to carve
himself up a nice hunk of juicy, rare
oatmeal, when suddenly the Nerd Phone
rings.

Excuse me, your phone is ringing.
Excuse me, your phone is ringing.
(So what'd you expect a
Nerd Phone to sound like?)

After fumbling and dropping it five
or six times (hey, he's a brain, not
an athlete), he scoops it out of the
oatmeal and answers:

"SuperGeeks R Us.
If it's boring and brainy,
not to call us would be a shame-y."
(Okay, so he's no poet, either.)

"Chester C., you've got the phone upside down
again."
"I'm sorry," our hero shouts.
"You'll have to speak up."
"Turn the phone around!"
"Listen, if you can't talk any
louder, I'll have to——"
"TURN THE PHONE AROUND! TURN THE PHONE AROUND! TURN
THE . . ."
In a flash of superhero superthought,
our superhero turns the phone around
and immediately recognizes the voice.
"Mr. President, is that you?"

"Of course it's me. Who else would be calling you to start up these superhero stories? Listen, Chester C., I've got some terrible news."

"The stores are all out of pocket protectors?" our hero asks.

"It's worse than that!"

"Somebody from the A.V. Club wants to join the football team?"

"No, it's even worse!"

"Sir, the only possible thing worse than that would be ..."

Ta-Da-DAAA ...

"Oh, no, sir, I'd recognize that bad-guy music anywhere. Don't tell me, is it—"

"That's right," the President answers. "Your archrival, 2-Kool 4 U, has just escaped from the Prison for the Criminally Colder than Cold. Not only that but ..."

Suddenly, our hero hears a booming bass throbbing through his phone. "Mr. President, what's that noise? What's going on? Mr. President?"

"That's my name, Lame,
so don't be puttin' it to shame."

"Huh? Mr. President, what's going on?"
The bass beat grows louder and
louder as the president continues to
speak:

"So this is the truth
I be layin' on you chump.
2-Kool has created
a chemical to dump."

"Mr. President, why are you talking
in rhyme?"

"He's poured it in the water
that we all be a-drinkin'
and it makes us so cool
that we no longer be a-thinkin'."

"No offense, sir, but that is some
of the worst poetry I've ever heard."

"This ain't no poetry,
don't be a sap.
Use yer brain, for a change,
what yer hearin' is rap."

"Holy hipster," our hero shouts.
"Are you telling me...sir, is he
somehow taking over the world with
his coolness?"

"Pierced bodies and brows,
shades so dark you can't see.
Tattoos all over our bods
like we're all on MTV.

"Yer the only one to help us
so don't be no fool.
Only yer supernerd powers
can free us from Kool."

"Yes, sir, I understand," our hero
shouts. "I'll get right on it!"
In a flash he slams the phone down
on his hand (just 'cause he's going
to save the world doesn't mean his
coordination has improved) and races
toward the window while, of course,
getting tangled up in the cord, which
means

K-lang, K-Bang
K-lang, K-Bang

dragging the phone all the way across the room with him.

Once he arrives, he looks outside. It's worse than he suspects. Everyone is smoking, wearing black clothes, mouthing off to their parents. It's worse than Friday night at the mall. Well, maybe not that bad, but close.

And since he's obviously cool-proof (there's no way anyone like Chester C. can ever be hip), he knows he's the only one who can help. Quickly, he slips into his Nerd Cape (not, of course, without spraining an arm or two), races to his Nerd-Mobile (not, of course, without crashing into a wall or two), and takes off to save the—

K-RASH
splinter, splinter, splinter

Okay, next time he'll remember to open the garage door before saving the day. But he's barely out on the street when, suddenly—

"Hey, McDoogle?" It was Cowboy Roy standing in the doorway to our little six-man bunkhouse.

"Yes, sir?"

"I suggest ya turn that contraption off and get some sleep."

I glanced down at my story. It was definitely getting interesting. "Can't you just give me a couple more—"

"It's up to you, but I figure you'll be needin' all the rest you can get . . . considerin' what I got planned fer ya tomorrow." He chuckled softly.

"Tomorrow?" I swallowed.

He chuckled louder. "Tomorrow."

I swallowed harder. "What's tomorrow?"

"Let's just say today was a holiday compared to what I've got planned fer ya little greenhorns tomorrow." With that, he shut the door. As he limped away, his little chuckles turned into out-and-out laughter. Talk about eerie. I suppose I should be happy that the man was finally starting to enjoy his job. But somehow I figured his idea of enjoyment wouldn't exactly be the same as mine.

Reluctantly, I reached over and shut Ol' Betsy down. Whatever Chester C. Chessclub was about to face would have to wait. I figure, if a person is gonna die, it's best he gets plenty of sleep the night before . . . so he's wide awake and doesn't miss any of the exciting details.

Little did I realize that dying might be a treat compared to what Cowboy Roy had in store. . . .

Chapter 2

What a Burn

"Okay, listen up!" Cowboy Roy shouted. White plumes of breath rose from his mouth as he rode back and forth in front of us in the corral. "Don't ask me why, but this mornin' I'm gonna try to teach you tenderfoots how to rope and brand them calves."

"What time is it?" Wall Street whispered from beside me.

"Just a couple hours before God gets up," I whispered back.

"Now I'm sure you greenhorns have been whinin' 'bout how hard I've been pushin' ya, but—"

"No, sir," a voice boomed out from the end of our line. "That's not true."

We all leaned forward to see Chad Diamond standing straight and tall in his brand-new cowboy hat and freshly pressed cowboy shirt.

"What's that?" Cowboy Roy asked.

"I'm just saying, sir, that if we're truly supposed to learn the fine art of being cowboys, you should be pushing us as hard as possible."

Opera and I exchanged looks of alarm.

Cowboy Roy turned his horse and trotted up to him. "How's that?"

"Yours is a noble profession, sir. And, if we are to properly appreciate its true value, we should be exposed to as much of your skill and expertise as possible."

"Oh, brother!" I groaned.

"What a jerk!" Opera moaned.

"Isn't he dreamy?" Wall Street sighed.

I gave her one of my looks, but she didn't catch it. She was too busy batting her eyelashes in Chad's direction, and he was too busy flexing his muscles in hers.

"So, you think I should be pushin' you harder?" Cowboy Roy asked.

"Yes, sir!"

Now, I'm not a violent guy (with my size and athletic ability, getting violent with somebody is basically like committing suicide), but if I were about two hundred pounds heavier, I'd have gone right over to Chad Diamond and pulled his never-before-used hat down over his overly used mouth.

Unfortunately, the guy still wasn't finished.

"And with Parents' Day coming up," he said, "the harder you push us, the more prepared we'll be to perform for them."

And then the most amazing thing happened. Cowboy Roy actually began to smile. Well, sort of. With all the years of disuse it was obvious his smiler was a little rusty. Truth be told, it looked more like he'd just sucked on a lemon, with his lips sort of half-grimacing, half-sneering. But it was a valiant attempt, and we all appreciated the effort.

What we did not appreciate was his answer: "Well, now"—he spat on the ground—"I think we can arrange to work you a little harder."

And what we appreciated even less was Chad's response: "That would be swell, sir. Just swell. I'm sure the sweatier we get, the happier we'll all be."

Once again, Chad threw a look over to Wall Street. Once again, she threw a look over to him. And me? Forget about throwing looks—I just wanted to throw up.

* * * * *

"I don't get it," I said to Opera as I gathered our ropes and headed into the arena, where a fire was heating up the irons to brand the calves. "What does she see in him?"

Opera shrugged. "Maybe a better question is, what does he see in her? I know Wall Street is our friend and everything, but Mr. Heart Throb over there could take his pick of any of these girls."

I glanced around the corral and had to admit he was right. Not that I'm an expert on girls (it's hard to be an expert on anything that won't give you the time of day), but when it comes to all the superficial stuff that superficial guys like Chad Diamond look for . . . well, let's face it, Wall Street would never be superficial enough for him. So what gives?

I looked back to the fire. Chad and Wall Street sat on the gate above it, the gate that penned in Satan Breath, the ranch's one and only bull. Yes sir, Charmin' Chad had definitely shifted into superflirt, and poor Wall Street was falling for it big-time.

"Okay, McDoogle," Cowboy Roy shouted, interrupting my nausea. "You're up next. Just rope one of them calves there and bring it over to get branded."

I nodded. It sounded simple enough. Just open up the lasso like this, just twirl it over my head like so, and just throw it over the nearest calf's head like—

"Not the fence post, McDoogle!" Cowboy Roy shouted. "The calf, throw it over the calf!"

I nodded, retrieved the rope, and tried again. My throw was closer, but not close enough.

"Not Opera, McDoogle! The calf! The calf!"

(Some people can be so picky.)

After unlassoing Opera, I tried a third time and . . . miracle of miracles . . . I succeeded. Yes sir, I threw that rope right over the calf's head. It was a work of art . . . well, except for the part of getting my leg tangled up in the middle of the rope . . . and the part where the calf decided to take a few laps around the corral, which, of course, meant I took a few laps, too.

"Dig in your heels!" Cowboy Roy shouted. "Dig in your heels!"

I tried to obey, but it's hard digging in your heels when you're bouncing on your head.

"Dig in!!"

"I'm'm'm'm try-ing-ing-ing-ing to-to-to-to . . . ," I shouted, bouncing behind the calf like a basketball on too much caffeine.

Suddenly, I had a brainstorm . . . well, more like a brainsquall . . . okay, more like a brain on a slightly cloudy day. The point is, I figured why don't I make a slipknot on the other end of the rope and lasso the nearest passing fence post to bring us to a stop.

A pretty good plan, if I do say so myself. And it would have worked . . . except that it took half a day to tie the knot (hey, you try tying knots while bouncing on your head), and another half a day to finally rope the fence.

The good news was, I finally succeeded. The bad news was, well, that I finally succeeded. I lassoed the fence all right. Unfortunately, the fence was actually the gate to Satan Breath's pen.

The kids on the gate all screamed and leaped off, scattering like cockroaches in a Raid commercial. Well, most of them scattered. It seems Chad had a little something extra to do first . . . a little something extra like reaching over and unlatching the gate!

What?? I couldn't believe my eyes! What was he doing!?

Suddenly, Satan Breath's gate flew open, and the big bull bolted out. He thundered into the arena, shaking the ground as he ran. After taking a lap or two he snorted and slowed to a stop. That's when he spotted me. He snorted again, shook his giant head, then gave a loud, rumbling:

"BROOOOO . . ."

I'm not exactly sure what he meant since I don't speak bull, but somehow I suspected he wasn't saying, "Hi, there. Wanna be my pal?"

So there I was, still caught in the rope, stretched

between a calf running in one direction and the gate that had opened in the other. Talk about being strung out, talk about being a sitting duck, talk about giving new meaning to the term "Bull's-eye."

The huge animal slowly lowered his head. He began to snort some more—harder, louder.

In the distance I could hear Cowboy Roy shouting, "McDoogle, get out of there! Get out of there!" I threw a look to him. He was on the other side of the fence, afraid in a major lawsuit kind of way.

Next, Satan Breath began to paw the ground—stomping and snorting. And finally, just to make things even more interesting, he decided to . . .

CHARGE!

Which, of course, forced me to

"AUGH!"

Which forced Cowboy Roy to shout even louder, "McDoogle, get out of there! Get out of there!"

"Help me!" I yelled. "Help me!"

It was obvious the man wanted to help, but for some reason he wouldn't enter the arena. Instead, he began to pace. "McDoogle!" Back and forth along the fence he paced like some caged animal, all the while yelling, "McDoogle!"

And then it happened. Somehow, some way, I was able to get my foot untangled from the rope. The good news was, I tore out of that arena faster than a cheap pair of blue jeans. The bad news was, I wasn't exactly paying attention to where I was tearing.

"Look out for the fire!" Opera shouted. "Wally, look out for the—"

K-rash! K-smash!
k-"ouch, ouch, ouch"

Yes sir, I raced right through the branding-iron fire, tripping and kicking those red-hot irons in all directions. I even managed to kick one or two in with me as I stumbled out of the arena and into Satan Breath's now-empty pen.

And still, Cowboy Roy was too frightened to help. But not Wall Street. She leaped over the gate, into the pen, and quickly shut it before Satan Breath could reenter.

Unfortunately, my little adventure wasn't quite over. Not just yet. There was still one more sound effect to go.

K-SSSSSSsssssss . . .

That, of course, is the sound a branding iron makes when it's been kicked out of the fire, and the kicker accidentally falls backward onto it— causing it to burn through his pants and into his rear.

That's right, the calves weren't the only ones branded that day.

And my rear wasn't the only thing burning. 'Cause as I looked over to Chad Diamond, thinking how he'd set me up, I was definitely smoking in a major kind of way.

Chapter 3

Shake, Rattle, and Yikes!

I'd had enough. Oh, I know what the Bible says about forgiving your enemies, and that we're not supposed to try to get even—but what does the Bible know about bucking broncos, branding irons, and Chad Diamond?

And, as far as I could tell, there's no place where it says I can't collect a couple of snakes in the middle of the night, sneak up to my enemy's window, and let those snakes loose inside his room. So . . . at the moment, Opera and I were busy climbing up the steep rocks behind the bunkhouses to find Chad a couple of little surprises. It might have been easier if

BONK!
"Ow, my shin!"

it wasn't so dark and

BONK!
"Ow, my other shin!"

one of us had remembered to bring a flashlight. But it seemed a small price to pay to get even with Charmin' Chad.

"Wally, are you sure this is going to work out?" Opera asked as we made our way up the steep rocks.

At first, I wasn't going to answer him. *"Work out?"* What a ridiculous question. Hasn't this guy read *any* of my books? But by the quiver in his voice I could tell he was getting pretty emotional, so I did my best to calm him.

"Don't worry," I said. "Some of the guys saw a nest of harmless garter snakes up here yesterday. All we have to do is grab a couple of them, toss them into this bag, and let them loose in Chad's cabin."

"And all I have to do is shake these Mexican maracas here, so he thinks they're rattlesnakes?" Opera asked. His voice was even more emotional than before. In fact, it almost sounded like he was about to cry.

"That's right," I said, "that's all you have to do. Then we'll see how brave the great Chad Diamond is."

Opera let out a loud sniff. Something was really

eating at him. Finally, I turned to him and asked, "Are you okay?" In the faint moonlight, I saw big tears streaming down his cheeks. "Listen," I said, "if this bothers you that much, I can do it on my own."

"It's not that," he quietly sobbed.

"Then what?" I asked.

He pointed to his Walkman, which he'd been playing extra soft. "It's this song."

"What opera are you listening to this time?"

"It's no opera." He sniffed. "It's worse."

"What could be worse than those sappy-sad operas you're always listening to?"

He burst out blubbering, "This sappy-sad, country-western song."

I looked at him and blinked. "You're kidding."

He shook his head. Tears kept pouring from his eyes, and his bottom lip was trembling like Jell-O on a jackhammer.

"Opera, you've been listening to classical music all of your life."

He nodded. "I know. But I thought country-western would help get me into the mood out here."

"And?" I asked.

Without a word he ripped off his headphones and gave me a listen. I couldn't believe my ears. It was true, he'd actually found music worse than opera. At the moment some woman was singing some typical *my-no-good-man-has-run-off-with-my-sister-in-his-pickup-with-the-nice-shiny-gun-rack-I-just-gave-him-for-our-anniversary-before-I-could-tell-him-I-was-gonna-have-our-baby-who-I'd-name-after-him-no-matter-how-bad-he-treats-me* song. You know the type.

And before I knew it, I, too, was starting to tear up.

"Isn't it sad?" Opera sobbed.

"It's worse than sad," I cried. "It's awful."

Opera nodded, sniffing and wiping his nose. Soon, we were both crying like babies.

"Please," I finally gasped, "in the name of all that is good and decent, please turn it off. *Turn it off!*"

Opera fumbled with the switch, and finally shut it down. "Really gets to you, doesn't it?" he asked.

I nodded, trying to catch my breath. "I'll say. And the scariest thing of all . . ."

"What's that?"

"I was starting to like it."

Opera nodded. "I know what you mean."

I took a deep breath to clear my mind (or whatever was left of it), and focused my attention back to our mission of finding those snakes.

"Wally," Opera pointed. "Over there."

I followed his finger to a crevice just above us and to our left.

"All right!" I said. I climbed up the remaining few feet. It was a small opening, not big enough for a normal person to squeeze into, but just right for us subnormal types like myself.

"Be careful," Opera warned.

The clouds had parted, and there was just enough moonlight to see into the crevice. I could spot the little critters lying peacefully, sound asleep. Kinda cute in a creepy sort of way.

"See anything?" Opera asked.

"Looks like a bunch of little ones," I said. "But no momma."

"Well, grab a couple, and let's get down from here."

"I was hoping for something bigger."

"Wally . . ."

"Oh, all right."

I reached in and very carefully grabbed one near its tail. Even though I'd been told they were harmless garter snakes, I figured it wouldn't hurt to be careful, just in case. I lifted the thing into the moonlight. It was definitely asleep, which was definitely okay with me.

"Careful, Wally, careful."

"No sweat," I said, pretending to sound calm as I opened the sack and casually dropped it in.

I reached back into the crevice and grabbed another one by the tail. It was just as asleep as its brother (or sister), and I was just as grateful. I dropped it into the sack as well.

"That's enough," Opera whispered.

"There's two or three left."

"Wally, that's enough."

I wanted to agree and get out of there, but I also wanted to give Chad the scare of a lifetime. So, even though it was against my better judgment, I reached in for a third.

"Wally!"

I quickly pulled it out. But this one was starting to wake up. It was slowly twisting and curling.

"Drop it in the bag!" Opera whispered.

I didn't have to be told twice. I was more than happy to drop it in with the others and close the sack. Then, slinging the bag over my shoulder, I said, "Come on, let's get out of—

"AUGHhhhh!"

That last word was supposed to be "here," but sometimes it's hard to remember all the words when your feet are busy slipping and you're busy

bounce, bounce,
tumble, tumble
sprain a foot here, break a neck there

falling down a steep, rocky slope.

The good news was, the fall didn't last forever. Even better news was, I managed to hold
the sack high over my head so the little critters
wouldn't get squished. And by the time Opera
(who insisted upon taking a slower route down)
joined me, I'd pretty much regained consciousness and set most of my broken bones.

"You okay?" he asked, offering me his hand
and helping me up.

"Sure," I said, glancing to the ground and check-
ing for any vital organs that might have popped
out. When I was sure nothing too important was
missing, I took a deep breath, threw the sack over
my shoulder, and said, "Come on, let's get going."

As we headed toward Chad's cabin I began to
chuckle. "This is going to be great," I said, "just
great."

Opera agreed. I could tell he was really getting into it by the way he started practicing
shaking the maracas.

We arrived under Chad's window. "All right," I
whispered as I set the sack on the ground behind
me and turned to the window. "All I have to do is
push up the window like so . . ." It gave a quiet
squeak, then opened easily.

"Wally," Opera whispered. He was really
going to town with shaking those maracas.

"Now hand me the sack."

"Wally?"

"You're doing fine," I whispered. "Just keep shaking those maracas and—"

"Wally?"

"What?" I turned toward him.

"I'm not shaking any maracas."

"What?"

He motioned to the maracas that he held motionless in his hands.

"Well, if you're not making the sound, then . . ."

He pointed to the sack between us. I frowned and picked it up, opening it for a look inside. The snakes were wide awake now, and by the look of things they weren't terribly happy. You could tell by the way they writhed, slithered, and rattled.

"AND RATTLED?!"

That's right, the little critters were anything but pleased . . . and they were anything but garter snakes!

I gave the world's second biggest scream (the first is over on page 47) and set off to break the land speed record. Unfortunately, I forgot one minor little detail.

"Wally, Wally!" Opera shouted.

"What, what?" I yelled.

"The bag! The bag!"

"What about it?"

"Drop it!"

(Hey, a guy can't remember everything.) As I glanced at it, I saw its insides were churning like a blender gone berserk. And being the type who always listens to his friends, I took Opera's advice. I threw down the bag and ran like the wind. It wasn't until we got back into our bunkhouse and locked the door that I decided to work a little something else into my scream-and-flee routine.

A little something else like, oh, I don't know . . .

"Ahhh . . ."
K-Thud

passing out.

"Wally . . . Wally, wake up." Opera kept shaking and yelling at me. "Wally!?"

But it did no good. I wasn't exactly dead, but I wouldn't exactly be waking up for a while, either.

Chapter 4

Friend or Foe?

When I finally decided to regain consciousness it was somewhere around 3:30 in the morning.

If you'd have guessed I was a little upset about nearly being bitten by the rattlesnakes, you would have guessed wrong. I wasn't a little upset, I was a *lot* upset. But instead of admitting that I was really the one to blame and that it was really my fault for seeking revenge, I did what I always do when I want to forget my troubles. I reached down and pulled out Ol' Betsy. Yes sir, nothing beats a little superhero story when you're trying to relax and unwind (not to mention avoid the blame) . . .

When we last left Chester C. Chess-club he was speeding down the road in his Nerd-Mobile to find the unbearably

hip and happening huckster (insert
bad guy music here ...).

Ta-Da-DAAAAA ...

Thank you.... The unbearably hip and
happening huckster: 2-Kool4 U!

Ta-Da-DAAAAA ...

Uh, thank you, we heard it the
first time.

"I know, but I just got some brand-new notes
that I wanted to try. What do you think?"

Wait a minute, you're not supposed
to talk, you're just the music guy.

"I know, but after eighteen books I
ought to be able to say something."

Sorry, I do the talking, you just
do the music.

"Why do you get all the fun?"

'Cause they're *my* stories.

"You don't have to get all huffy about it."

`I'm not getting—`

"If you ask me, your head's been getting
          pretty big lately."

`Please, would you just—`

"And I'm not the only one who thinks so."

`Look, we're running out of pages
here. I've got to get back to my
story—`

> `K-Rash, K-Bang, K-Pow`
> `tinkle, tinkle, tinkle ...`

`Oh, brother, now it's Sound Effects
Guy. And what do you want?`

"I just want to (*K-Bamb, K-Boom*) agree with
          Music Guy here. You really are
          (*K-Bounce, K-Bounce, K-Bounce*)
          getting kinda bossy lately."

`Please, guys, can we get back to my
story?`

"Oh, so now it's (*K-Pop*) *your* story."

"You see, that's exactly what we're
(*Ta-Da-Daaaaa*) talking about."

"All right, I'm sorry, I'm sorry.
You're right, it's *our* story. But can
we discuss it later? Please?

"Well, o(*K-Bing*)kay."

"But don't forget."

I won't, I promise. Now, where was
I? Oh yeah, no one's sure why or how
2-Kool first got too cool. Some say
it was from riding around in his
brother's car with those big bass
speakers pounding away. Others say it
came when his baby-sitter kept pop-
ping *Grease* into their VCR and watching it over and over again. Then
there's the ever-popular theory that
it was simply an allergic reaction to
too many Teletubbies reruns.
Whatever the reason, 2-Kool became
too cool to be safe. And now he is
trying to take over the world with

his horrendous hipness by polluting
the drinking water.

But how is it possible? How could
one villain be contaminating all of
the world's water supply? How could
one bad guy, no matter how bad, reach
every well and reservoir in the world?
Unless ...

Great garbanzo beans! In a flash of
incurable intellectual intelligence,
Chester C. has it figured out. 2-Kool
isn't contaminating the water by dump-
ing chemicals into it. No, of course
not. He's changing the subatomic
makeup of H_2O's hydrogen atom through
hyperinductive neutron vibration.

(I'm sure most of you knew that,
but I had to explain it for the
younger readers.)

Which can only mean ...

          Ta-Ta-Taaaaa ...

What's that?

       "Realization music."

Thanks, don't need it. Which can

only mean our villainous villain is
hiding out in the depths of the
Earth. Then, with even more expert
calculations, our hero—

Ta-Ta—

Don't need that, either.

"Sorry."

Then, with even more expert calculations (by
the way, I'm typing this smaller and closer together so no music or sound effects can be squeezed
in), our hero calculates the exact location.

Suddenly, and with complete lack of coordination (not to mention driving skills), Chester
C. spins his Nerd-Mobile around (three or
four more times than necessary),while, of course,
wiping out one stop sign, two mailboxes, and don't
even ask about that poor little rabbit trying to
cross the road (though the Nerd-Mobile suddenly
looks a lot better with its new live-animal hood
ornament).

Soon he is heading toward the largest cavern in
the country. Carl's-*REALLY*-Bad Cavern!

Who knows what creepy concoctions the criminally cool kid can cook up?

Who knows what kind of crazy caper the creepy
culprit can create?

Who knows how many more *c* words I can come up
with?

(Who cares?)

And what about the music and sound effects guys?
Are they going to keep coming back and interrupting the story?

"Maybe."

"And (*K-Blewy*), maybe not."

Oh, brother. Then, suddenly, out of
the blue—

Ol' Betsy's screen went blank.

What on Earth? I pressed the power button
and nothing happened.

I pressed it again.

Repeat in the nothing department. It was
only then that I realized the battery was dead.

Great, I thought, *just great. I spend all that
time arguing with the music and sound guys
and now I have no power left for the story.* It
looked like I'd have to do a little battery re-

charging first. And, speaking of recharging, as I closed Ol' Betsy's screen, I thought it might not be a bad idea to get a little rest myself. Tomorrow was going to be a busy day.

Little did I realize that all the rest in the world wouldn't prepare me for what was about to happen. . . .

* * * * *

"All right, Buckaroos, listen up."

It was early morning, and once again Cowboy Roy was pacing back and forth in front of us like an army drill sergeant. You'd never know this was the same man who had been so frightened of Satan Breath yesterday. And, since we all felt like living another day or so, none of us felt a need to mention it to him.

"Parents' Day is in two days." He leaned over his horse and spit on the ground. "And as is our custom, we'll be putting on a little rodeo for them."

"Little rodeo, sir?" Chad Diamond asked in a too-chipper-for-the-morning voice.

"That's right," Cowboy Roy said. "Now, it's important that ya make a good impression on them so they see what fine, outstanding young men and women each of ya has become."

I couldn't believe my ears. Was Cowboy Roy actually paying us a compliment?

"Of course, you and me know that's all hogwash, but as long as they think it, they'll dish out the money for ya to come again next year."

So much for compliments.

"Now, I've assigned each of ya an event. For some of ya it will be calf roping, for others barrel racing or bronco riding—just like a real, honest-to-goodness rodeo. Any questions?"

"Yes, sir," Opera said. "I was just wondering—"

"Good," Cowboy Roy cut him off. "Then saddle up and drag yer sorry selves over to the arena. We'll be starting in thirty minutes."

Twenty-nine and a half minutes later, when I was still trying to saddle up Ol' Bag a Bones, Chad Diamond came trotting up to me on his horse while pulling another behind him. "Hey, Wally."

"What do you want?" I tried to sound mean and tough. And I might have pulled it off, if—

"O-Oaf!"
K-plop

I wasn't suddenly spread-eagle on the ground with the saddle on top of me. The best I could figure Ol' Bag a Bones was going for a record in the number of times she could sidestep me as I tried to throw the saddle on her.

Chad answered, "I just want to say I'm sorry 'bout that bull thing yesterday."

I looked up at him. "What do you mean?"

"I mean, when I leaped off the gate. I'm sorry, my hand accidentally caught the latch and I unlocked the pen."

"You're telling me it was an accident?"

Chad nodded, obviously embarrassed. "It was a stupid accident and I'm really sorry."

I couldn't believe my ears. Had I really misjudged him? Had it really been an accident? Had I nearly filled his room with live rattlers for no reason at all? Talk about feeling stupid. Here I was trying to get revenge when it had been nothing but a mistake all along.

"Hey," I said, crawling out from under the saddle. "Don't worry about it. I do that sort of stuff all the time."

"You do?"

"Oh yeah, but it usually involves dinosaur skeletons falling down or crash landing space shuttles and stuff."

"No kidding?"

"Yeah," I said, suddenly beginning to feel that we might actually have something in common.

"Well, just to let you know I'm sorry, I saddled

up this horse for you. Cowboy Roy said he's a lot easier to ride and not nearly as stubborn as Ol' Bag a Bones." He handed the reins down to me.

"You did that for me?" I asked.

"Sure, just to say I hope there're no hard feelings."

"Well, no, of course not." I reached down to the other saddle on the ground, but Chad was already off his horse and moving to pick it up.

"Here, let me get that," he said.

"No, that's—"

"No, really, it's the least I can do."

I watched as Chad heaved the saddle up into his arms and headed for the tack room to put it away. I guess I really was wrong about the guy. I turned to my new horse, put my foot in the stirrup, and after ten or fifteen tries finally managed to get up into the saddle.

Chad was right, he was a great horse. Strong. Obedient. We seemed to hit it off right away.

"Hey, Chad," I called as he came back out of the tack room. "What's his name?"

"His?" Chad asked as he mounted his own horse and eased into the saddle.

"Yeah."

"Undertaker."

I frowned. "Undertaker? Why do they call him that?"

Chad reached over toward my horse's flank. "'Cause everybody who rides him eventually sees the undertaker."

"Yeah, right," I chuckled. "Actually, this horse is as gentle as—"

"YEE-HAAA!"
SLAP
"AUGHHHHHHHhhhhhh . . ."

The "YEE-HAAA!"—if you hadn't already guessed—was Chad suddenly yelling at my horse.

The *SLAP* was Chad suddenly slapping my horse.

And the "AUGHHHHHHHhhhhhh . . ." was me letting loose the world's biggest scream (even bigger than page 34), and clinging to Undertaker for dear life . . . as he began leaping and bucking.

Oh, and there was one other sound amid all the yelling and slapping and screaming . . .

The sound of Chad Diamond laughing his head off.

Chapter 5

An I for an Eye

So there we were, running, jumping, leaping, and

BUCK "Whoa!"
BUCK "Whahhhhh!"
BUCK "EEEEEEEEEE!"

Well, actually, Undertaker was doing most of the running, jumping, and leaping. I was too busy yelling and hanging on for my life. Then, when we got tired of those fun and games, we tried something entirely different. Something that sounded an awful lot like:

"AUGHHHHHHH. . ."
(that's me flying through the air)

followed by

"AUGhhhhhhhh..."
(that's me coming back down again)

And what gymnastic routine would be complete without the grand finale—a good healthy and hearty:

K-SPLAT

Now, the more attentive reader will notice this is identical to the sound effect on page 2 when I landed in the world's biggest manure pile. And there is a very simple explanation:
IT IS THE SAME MANURE PILE!
(Sorry, didn't mean to yell.)

But like I always say, if something is worth doing, it's worth doing well. This time I dove in so deep that I couldn't even see daylight. Then, after a couple of eternities, I began to hear, ever so faintly:

"Wawee...?"

What was that?

"Wawee... Waa ooo okaa?"

Was someone trying to communicate with me?

"Wawee..."

But why were they talking in a strange, foreign language?

"Wawee, aanwher mee."

Maybe they were aliens from another planet.
Or another dimension. Or—

"Wawee . . ."

And then I felt it . . . a hand grabbing my leg
and trying to pull me out. After several attempts,
I finally popped out of the pile like a cork from a
bottle. I tell you, it was great to finally see daylight again. (And the part about being able to
breathe wasn't too bad, either.)

"Wawee . . ."

I turned and to my surprise saw that it was
Wall Street who had saved me.

"Waa ooo okaa?" she asked.

I frowned, trying to understand.

"Wawee . . . waa ooo okaa?"

Finally, she pointed to my ears and motioned
for me to clean them out. Not a bad idea. And,
after removing two or three pounds of . . . well,
you know . . . from each ear, I was able to hear.

"Oh, Wally," she practically sobbed, "I was so
scared. Are you okay?"

I shrugged. "Yeah, I think so."

"I had no idea," she continued. "When I helped
Chad saddle up Undertaker for you, I didn't expect—"

"You helped Chad?" I asked in astonishment.

"Well, yes. We wanted to give you a horse
with a bit more spunk."

"You were in with him on this?"

"Yes," she repeated. "But it wasn't supposed to end like this."

"I can't believe it," I said. "You actually helped him?"

She reached out to me. "Wally—"

But I shook her off. Then I turned and started to hobble away.

She was right at my side. "Wally, I'm sorry. I had no idea."

"Yeah, right."

She blinked in surprise. "What?"

I said nothing, letting my words sink in.

"You don't . . ." She swallowed. "Wally, you don't think . . ." She tried a third time. "You don't think we planned for this to happen?"

I turned to her and in my lowest, coolest voice said, "You tell me."

It had just the effect I wanted, causing her mouth to drop open to her knees. Without a word, I turned and continued hobbling off.

She called after me. "Wally? Wally?!"

But I kept right on hobbling. I didn't know what was going on, but I was going to show her. And I was going to show that precious Chad Diamond of hers, too.

I was going to show everyone.

* * * * *

By the time I got to the arena, Cowboy Roy was already passing out the assignments. No surprises, really. The real athletic guys like Chad got calf roping—a cool thing where they gallop up to a calf on their horse, rope it, then jump down to tie up its legs in the shortest amount of time. Luckily, I wasn't on that list . . . because even though I'd break all the records for the shortest amount of time, I'd be the one who got my legs tied up.

Next came broncobusting, where you ride a bucking horse. And, despite all of my experience, Cowboy Roy didn't put me with that group, either. (Proof there's a loving God in heaven.)

After that came barrel racing. Wall Street and some others got that. I have to admit I kinda wanted it, too, since I knew even I could beat a barrel in a race. It wasn't until I learned that it involved racing horses around the barrels that I was glad my name wasn't called.

"And finally, least but not last," Cowboy Roy said, "this year's clown is . . . Wally McDoogle!"

The cheers weren't exactly deafening. And the applause, well, it wasn't exactly audible. But there was plenty of snickering. And giggling. Lots of giggling. Still, I wasn't put off. No way. I figured they were just jealous 'cause they wouldn't get to walk around in absurd-looking clothes, and wear huge, embarrassing-looking shoes, or be totally humiliated by putting on stupid clown makeup. And let's not forget the big, moron-looking, red nose. I mean, who in their right mind wouldn't want to wear a big, moron-looking, red nose in front of their parents and hundreds of strangers?

Needless to say, I left the meeting more than a little depressed. Fortunately, I had Opera to cheer me up.

"Hey, don't, *crunch, crunch,* take it too bad," he said, joining me as we headed toward our various practice areas.

"Why not?" I asked.

"Falling down, looking stupid, and making a total fool of yourself . . . at least you won't have to practice. I mean, you've been doing that all your life."

"Thanks," I muttered.

"No problem, *munch, munch*. What are friends for?"

"What about you?" I asked as I watched him dip a chip into another jar of Pecos Bill's Flame Thrower Hot Sauce. "I didn't hear your name called."

"That's 'cause I've got a special assignment," he beamed.

"Special assignment?"

"That's, *burp*, right."

"Like what?"

"I'm in charge of the concession, *BELCH* (*wow, that was a good one*), cart."

I nodded, cranking up a little smile. Good ol' Cowboy Roy. He really had a knack for knowing our strengths. "Hey," I asked, "is that Chad's horse over there?"

"Yup. The calf ropers are heading to the barn to learn to tie different knots and stuff. Why?"

"Oh, no reason," I said.

But, of course, there was a reason. And as soon as Opera left for his concession cart training, I sneaked back to the horses. If Chad wanted to play hardball, I could play hardball. A little eye for an eye never hurt anybody (though so far I seemed to be the only one going blind). But that would all change. Very, very soon that would change.

It took only a minute to loosen the saddle's cinch on his horse . . . not too much, just enough so it would gradually slip and come undone. When I was finished, I shoved my hands into my pockets, whistled a happy tune, and strolled over to the little trailer where they were going to measure me for my clown outfit.

Yes sir, things were going to turn around in no time. Little did I realize how turned around they would become. . . .

Chapter 6

A Goof for a Goof

The person in charge of measuring me for my clown costume was Mrs. Cowboy Roy. I know, as impossible as it is to believe, there actually was a *Mrs.* Cowboy Roy. And, even more impossible to believe, she looked and acted exactly like her husband . . . well, except for the spitting part. No way would you catch this fine lady spitting on the ground.

She used a cup.

To call it a "measuring" was a bit of a stretch. Basically, it involved Mrs. Cowboy Roy throwing the clothes at me from an old trunk (apparently, one size fits all) and ordering me to go into the back room to put them on.

I won't bore you with the details of my new wardrobe. Just imagine bright green pants slightly larger than a water barrel (but not nearly as comfortable), bright red suspenders (industrial-sized to hold up my water-barrel-sized pants), socks that stretch up somewhere around my earlobes, and a big shirt with yellow and purple stripes so ugly it's probably outlawed in most states, except California. Then, of course, there was the battery-powered bow tie. By pressing a button in my pants it would light up a bright red and begin to spin. In short, it wasn't exactly the type of stuff you'd want to wear to church. In long, it wasn't exactly the type of stuff you'd want to wear anywhere.

"So, how do I look?" I asked as I stepped back into the room.

Mrs. Cowboy Roy glanced up, then spit into her cup. "Just as stupid as last year's clown."

"Thanks," I said.

"'Course, you'll look even more ignorant with the clown makeup."

"Oh, boy."

"And"— she spat again—"the bright red nose."

"You mean this big moron-looking nose?" I asked, holding a red rubber ball that had been cut in half.

"That's the one."

"Great," I moaned.

"But that bow tie is pretty cool," she said.

I nodded, having to admit she was right. I pushed the button in my pants, causing the tie to light up and start spinning around.

"That's what Roy used to use to attract the bulls in the rodeo," she said.

"Cowboy Roy used to be a rodeo clown?" I asked.

"One of the best," she said as she spit. "Till he got hurt. Never been the same since."

"What happened?"

"Some bull rider got throwed, and Roy jumped in to save him."

"He did?" I asked.

"Yup. He leaped smack dab in front of the animal."

"And . . ."

"And he got his attention, all right. The critter gored him with his horns, threw him to the ground, then nearly trampled him to death."

"That's terrible."

"Then he turned on the cowboy."

"What happened?"

"The kid didn't have a chance."

"You mean"—I swallowed—"the bull killed him?"

Mrs. Cowboy Roy nodded slowly. "'Course, everyone told Roy it weren't his fault . . . but to this day he holds himself responsible."

"That's why . . . Is that why he's so scared of Satan Breath?" I asked.

"That's right."

"But if he's so scared of bulls, why does he keep that one?"

"Need him for breeding," Mrs. Cowboy Roy said. "Can't have a cattle ranch, if you can't raise cattle." Then, more quietly, she added, "Not that it will be making all that much difference soon."

"What do you mean?"

Mrs. Cowboy Roy took a long breath, and I noticed her voice got kinda thick and emotional. "Somethin' in Roy died that day. He ain't never been the same." She reached out and cinched my pants up just a little higher than my eyebrows. Then she continued. "Don't you be tellin' him I told you or nothing, but every year we fall a little further behind in our payments for the ranch. Fact, running this camp for you kids is the only way we can make ends meet."

"Is that why . . . this Parents' Day rodeo thing is so important to him?"

She nodded. "To both of us. Bank is already closing in. If we don't get more campers, we'll be losing the ranch for sure."

"That's terrible," I said.

"Terrible or not, it's a reality." She reached back into the trunk. "Now here," she said, producing a pair of big floppy shoes, "put these on."

"But they're a hundred times too big."

"That's the idea," she said. She forced me to sit and shoved the first one onto my foot.

"I can't walk in these."

"You catch on fast," she said, shoving on the other. "Half the fun is seeing the clown stagger around the arena making a total fool of himself."

I was about to point out that, being Wally McDoogle, I didn't need a pair of shoes to do that, when Opera suddenly banged on the trailer door. "Hey, Wally! Wally, you in there?"

I stood and walked over to the

> *Flip-flop . . . fall*
> *Flip-flop . . . fall*

. . . er, I stood and tried to walk over to the door. After the twenty-third time, I finally arrived and opened it.

"What's up?" I asked.

If his eyes had gotten any wider, you could have used them as headlights. Yes sir, my wardrobe definitely left him speechless. Not only speechless but chewless. For the first time that I could remember, Opera actually stopped chomping on his chips and hot sauce—but only for 1.8 seconds. Soon he started up again and found his voice.

"Cool," he said. "Do you get to keep the tie?"

"What's up?" I repeated.

"Wall Street's 'bout to start her barrel racing thing. Thought you'd want to see."

I turned to Mrs. Cowboy Roy, and she waved

me on. "Go ahead, we'll work on the wig and makeup tomorrow."

"Great," I sighed. "I can hardly wait." Closing the door behind me, I headed down the

Flip-flop . . .
tumble, tumble, tumble

stairs and ran

Flip-flop . . . fall
Flip-flop . . . fall

toward the arena.

As we approached, I could see that Wall Street was already starting to mount up. In front of her, out in the arena, were three big barrels. But it wasn't the barrels that grabbed my attention. It was Wall Street's horse. Well, it should have been Wall Street's horse. But it wasn't, it was Chad's. For some reason Chad had lent her his!

"No! Wall Street!"

"What's wrong?" Opera asked.

"She's on Chad's horse!" I cried.

"Yeah, he lent it to her 'cause it's faster."

"But . . ."

"What's up?"

"But . . . but . . ."

"Wally, you okay?"

"But . . . but . . . but . . ." I knew I could either continue my motorboat imitation or move into action. Unfortunately, I moved into action. Quickly, I raced toward the corral. (Well, as quickly as you can race in size thirty-seven shoes.)

Flip-flop . . . fall
Flip-flop . . . fall

"Wall Street, don't!"

She looked over to me, her smile fading. I wasn't sure if it was because of my clothes or our last little conversation.

"Don't do it!" I shouted. "Don't ride that horse!"

She turned her head and purposefully ignored me. (Well, at least I had my answer.) But I continued running

Flip-flop . . . fall

toward her. "Wall Street, don't!" I finally arrived at the arena and shouted over the fence. "Get off the—"

But that was all I said before she kicked her horse and took off racing out of the box. Dust and dirt flew as she charged toward the first barrel. She rounded it a little wide and started for the second one. But I wasn't watching the barrels. I was watching the horse. Actually, the saddle on the horse . . . Chad's horse.

Soon it began to happen. The saddle started to slip. At first no one noticed . . . except Wall Street. She tried to reposition herself as she approached the second barrel. She took the turn a little closer and tighter. Everyone cheered her on.

Well, everyone but me.

I watched in horror as the saddle kept slipping farther and farther to the side, as she kept readjusting herself, trying to hang on.

Everyone kept shouting and cheering.

The third barrel was directly in front of me, and as she galloped toward, it I started to yell and wave. "Wall Street!"

But again she ignored me.

And it was on that third and final turn that it happened. The saddle slipped all the way off and

"AUGH . . ."

For once in my life, the scream didn't belong to me. But in another sense, it did—because I was the whole reason she was crying out. I watched in horror as, like some slow-motion movie, she slipped off the horse and . . .

K-Thud

hit the ground.

"W-w-a-a-a-l-l-l . . . S-s-t-r-e-e-e-t . . ." (That, of course, was me yelling in slow motion.)

She tumbled and somersaulted across the dirt like a rag doll—once . . . twice . . . three . . . four times, before she finally rolled to a stop.

"Wall Street!" I leaped off the fence and raced into the arena after her.

> *Flip-flop . . . fall*
> *Flip-flop . . . fall*

That was my friend out there, my buddy. What had I done?!

"Wall Street!!!"

But she did not answer. She just lay on the ground not saying a word, not making a sound. Come to think of it, she wasn't making a move, either.

All this as I continued to

> *Flip-flop . . . fall*
> *Flip-flop . . . fall*

"Wall Street!! WALL STREET!!!"

Chapter 7

More Unforgiveness...

"Stand back, get out of the way!" Cowboy Roy pushed through the kids who were gathering around Wall Street. "Stand back!" We parted as Cowboy Roy arrived and kneeled down to her side. "Wall Street, can you hear me? Wall Street?!"

A couple hundred years passed (which may have been only a few seconds but it's hard to measure time when you've killed your best friend). Then, at last her eyes began to flutter and finally open.

"You okay, kid?" Cowboy Roy asked.

She took a deep, unsteady breath. Then she nodded. She tried to sit up, but it was obvious she was still too dizzy.

"Just lay back and rest," he said.

She nodded and looked up at all of the faces staring down at her. I was in luck 'cause her eyes didn't meet mine . . . not yet. When she finally spoke, her voice was like sandpaper washed down with a big glass of gravel. "What . . . happened?"

"Your saddle slipped off," he said. "You forgot to cinch it up tight."

A frown crossed her face. "Are you sure?" she croaked.

"'Course, I'm sure." Then, turning to the rest of us, he couldn't resist giving another lecture. "Ain't I always telling ya kids to keep stuff tight and double-check yer work?"

"But I did, sir." We all looked to Chad Diamond, who was standing a couple of kids from me. "That was my horse, and I cinched up that saddle real tight . . . I'm sure of it."

"Well, it didn't just fall off by itself," Cowboy Roy glowered.

The frown deepened on Wall Street's face as she looked around the group . . . until her eyes finally connected with mine. I tried to look away, but couldn't. Of course, she didn't know what I was thinking, but she would soon enough. Hey, she was my best friend. Just 'cause I tried to kill her, doesn't mean I could lie to her. . . .

* * * * *

"You did what?!" she cried, rising up from her bed.

"I, uh, I was the one who uncinched your saddle."

"You did what?" she repeated, not believing her ears.

"Well, actually, it wasn't your saddle. I uncinched Chad's saddle."

"You did what?"

"Listen, would you mind saying something else for a while?"

Unfortunately, she did: "Wally, you nearly killed me."

"I know, and I'm sorry. I wasn't trying to kill—"

"Well, you were sure doing a pretty good imitation of it!"

"But—"

"I know you're mad at me for hanging out with Chad—"

"But, but—"

"And you think we planned that thing with Undertaker—"

"But, but, but—"

"But that's no reason to try to hurt me."

Growing tired of another one of my motorboat imitations, I finally shouted, "I wasn't trying to hurt you, I was trying to hurt Chad!"

Her eyes widened in astonishment. "You were trying to hurt Chad?"

"Well, not hurt, really." I swallowed guiltily. "I just wanted to, you know, scare him a little."

She lay back down on her bed. Although Cowboy Roy had said she was all right, he had still wanted her to go back to her bunkhouse and rest for a while, which she had been only too happy to do.

Unfortunately, she was not so happy to hear my story.

I swallowed and continued nervously. "I mean, after all the stuff he's done to me, I just figured—"

"You still believe he's trying to be mean to you?"

I shook my head. "He's not trying, Wall Street, he's succeeding."

"So . . . you were going to get even," she said. "You were after revenge?"

"Well, uh, yeah. I mean, if you want to get technical about it."

She started to speak, then closed her mouth and shook her head.

I sat silently beside her, waiting.

But she said nothing.

I waited some more.

She said nothing some more.

The silence was killing me. She had to say something. Finally, after a couple thousand years, I cleared the cobwebs from my throat and said, "Listen, I'm really sorry. I know I messed up on this."

She said nothing even some more.

"I mean, I'm totally to blame. I really thought Chad had it in for me. And I guess, I mean, even if he did, I should have just let it go."

More silence.

"So, uh, well, I'm sorry. Okay?"

More silence some more.

"Okay?" I repeated.

And then, ever so slowly, she began to shake her head.

I frowned. "What do you mean?"

Her head continued to shake, harder. And the harder it shook the tighter my stomach got. Was she saying what I thought she was saying? I repeated, "Wall Street, what do you mean?"

At last she spoke. But, despite all of the silence, all of that time I had wanted her to talk . . . well, I would have given anything not to hear what she said. Her voice was a hoarse whisper. "Not this time, Wally. You've done some pretty stupid things in your life."

"I know," I croaked.

"And we've managed to stay friends through them all." She hesitated. I could tell this was almost as hard on her as it was on me. Then, after a deep breath she continued, "But not this time." She kept shaking her head, then she said the words even more quietly, her voice thick with emotion. "This time you've gone too far."

* * * * *

I walked out of her cabin absolutely numb. It was lunchtime, and everyone was over at the mess hall eating. Well, everyone but me. I just kept on thinking as I wandered around the buildings up on the hill above the corrals—well, actually, as I *flip-flopped* around the buildings up on the hill just above the corrals. (That's right, I'd never bothered to take off those goofy shoes.)

What had I done? How had everything gotten so out of hand?

Of course, I knew the answer before I asked. It was a simple word that started with the letters REV and ended in ENGE (with not a whole lot of letters in between). Revenge: what a terrible thing. It's like a wheel that just keeps spinning faster and faster until it's out of control and everything gets flung off. In this case the "everything" was one of the most important things . . . my friendship with Wall Street. Well, there was no doubt about it, I'd learned my lesson. From that moment on I would never seek revenge again. Never. And as soon as things got straightened out, I would—

Suddenly, I heard voices and slowed to a stop. They were around the storage shed just in front of me. Kids' voices. In fact, one of them sounded an awful lot like Chad Diamond. And the closer I got, the more I knew the reason:

It *was* Chad Diamond.

"I'm telling you guys," he was saying, "chicks are all the same. Show them a little attention and they go bonkers."

"You've done this before?" a second voice asked.

"All the time," he said. "Find some girl who thinks she has it all together, get her all worked up, then drop her and watch her shatter into a million pieces."

"Cool," a gravelly, third voice chuckled.

"Yeah," the second agreed.

"Gotta do something to pass the time," Chad said. "Hey, pass me the cigarette."

I couldn't believe my ears. I pressed against the shed's wall and moved in closer to hear better. Soon I was beside a bunch of empty fifty-five-gallon barrels.

"This time, though," Chad continued, "I've got myself a doubleheader."

"What do ya mean?" the second voice asked.

"That dork-oid with the glasses."

"Wally Mc-what's-his-name?" the gravelly voice asked.

"Yeah," Chad said. "The way I figure it, he and she are like best friends."

"So?" the second kid said.

"So, not only do I get to stomp on her heart, but if I play it right, I get to ruin their friendship, too."

Gravel Voice chuckled. "You're evil, dude, real evil."

"Thanks." There was a moment's silence as I heard him take what sounded like another drag from his cigarette.

"So when you gonna dump her?" the second voice asked.

"Tomorrow, at Parents' Day. I figure, let her get all excited about introducing me to Mommy and Daddy, and then when the big moment comes, I totally ignore her."

"Like you don't even know who she is," Gravel Voice said.

"Exactly."

"Cruel, real cruel."

"Yup," Chad said, "just the way I like it."

The other two kids chuckled in appreciation.

"Well, we better get back before they miss us," Chad said.

"Yeah," they agreed.

I could hear by the crunch of dirt under their feet that they were leaving. Unfortunately, they were leaving directly toward me! Now, the way I figured it, I had three choices.

<u>CHOICE ONE</u>: Stay there and confront Chad; you know, face to face, man to wimp. Tell him what I heard and that I wasn't going to let him do it. Of course, this was the best choice . . . except for all of his muscles, all of his friends' muscles, and my extreme allergy to being beaten to death. (I break out in a bad case of death every time it happens.) Look, it's not that I can't fight; I've fought with the best of them (it's just that my folks get real tired of paying for all those hospital bills).

<u>CHOICE TWO</u>: Run like the wind. Not bad except for my size thirty-seven clown feet.

<u>CHOICE THREE</u>: Hide. And since there were all these empty barrels around me, and since I could easily fit inside one . . .

Quicker than you can spell superchicken, I hopped into one of the open barrels. And just in time. I'd barely made it inside before the group rounded the corner and passed me.

Fortunately, no one bothered to look inside the barrels.

Unfortunately, it was my barrel that they decided to flick the cigarette butt into.

No problem . . . except for it landing on my clown shirt, which suddenly caught fire.

Even that would have been okay, if I'd just stayed quiet and burned up like a nice, well-behaved clown. But, being new to the clown business, I

"YEOW!"

didn't.

"What was that?" Gravel Voice asked.

"I don't know," Chad said. "It came from one of these barrels."

At first I paid them no attention. When you're busy swatting out flames all over your body, it's hard to notice the minor distractions. But when I finally got the last of the fire put out and looked up, I saw three very concerned faces gazing down at me.

"It's okay." I gave a nervous laugh. "I'm okay."

But, somehow, I got the impression that they weren't exactly concerned about my health.

"Well, well, well," Chad sneered. "What do we have here?"

"Uh, not much," I explained. "Just your typical clown in a barrel."

He leaned closer and leered down at me. "It wouldn't be the type of clown that spies and eavesdrops on people, would it?"

"Well, I, uh . . ." I figured it was time to stand up and explain. But I'd barely gotten to my feet before

K-WHOMP

Chad pushed the barrel (and me) over. Before I could catch my breath (or break into a good healthy scream), he gave it a good, hard

K-Thud

kick. And then

K-Thud

another. And

K-Thud

another.

Of course, I tried to scramble out and onto the ground, but just when I thought I knew where the ground was, it turned into the sky . . . and then the ground again . . . and then the sky. That's right, the ol' barrel and I were definitely on a roll . . . in more ways than one.

"Uh, guys . . ."

Roll, Roll . . .

" . . . listen, this is a lot of fun, but—"

Roll, Roll, Roll . . .

"—maybe if you let me get out I can help push and—"

Roll, Roll, Roll, Roll . . .
W-oooosh!

The good news was, I was done rolling. The bad news was, I was suddenly sailing. Sailing and

"AUGHHH!"

screaming. Lots and lots of screaming.

The best I could figure, they'd rolled me over the edge of the bluff, and by the way the sky and clouds were spinning around, I was momentarily airborne in a *"Mayday-Mayday-*

this-is-Wally-McDoogle-coming-in-for-a-crash-landing" kind of way.

And, sure enough, I . . .

K-RASH!

did just that.

Unfortunately the *K-RASH* didn't stop my *Roll*ing (or my "AUGHHH!"ing), but at least my flying days were over. At least I was back on the ground where I was safe and

K-RASH!

Wait a minute, didn't I already *K-RASH* hitting the ground? So, if I just *K-RASH*ed hitting the ground, then this other *K-RASH* must have come from running into something.

With that bit of Einstein logic, I poked my head outside of the rolling barrel. It was still the same view of the ground and sky, spinning around . . . only now it was ground and sky spinning around from inside a corral.

Oh, I get it. I'd *K-RASH*ed through a fence, and now I was rolling inside a—

K-thud.

Well, no, I wasn't rolling anywhere. Suddenly, I'd come to a dead stop. That was the good news. But as we all know, there's always some bad . . .

"BROOOO . . ."

I stuck my head back out of the barrel and took a peek. I'd hit something and come to a dead stop all right. Unfortunately, the word *dead* was more accurate than I wanted. Because that something wasn't a some*thing* but a some*one*. A someone with very sharp horns and very angry eyes—very sharp horns and angry eyes that looked exactly like they belonged to . . . Satan Breath.

"BROOOO . . ."

"Uh, hi there," I kinda half-squeaked. "Good to see you again."

Snort, snort . . .

He didn't look happy. But at least he wasn't pawing the ground. Because, from my last experience, I knew that when they paw the ground, you're in real—

Paw, paw . . .

Uh-oh. It looked like Satan Breath had something else on his mind. Something else that involved lowering his head and

Paw, paw . . .
trot, trot, trot
run, run, run, run

charging toward me and my Barrel Buddy full tilt!

"BROOOO!"

Finally, we

K-Bamb
"AUGHHH!"
roll, roll, roll . . .

connected. And then we

K-Bamb
"EEEEK!"
roll, roll, roll . . .

connected again.
Yes sir, it was great to get back into my

screaming and rolling routine. But, then, just when I was really getting the hang of it, he decided to try a new game. I wasn't sure of all the rules, but it involved sticking his horns inside the barrel, missing my ribs by a couple of inches, then lifting us up and hurtling us high into the air.

"AUGH . . ."

What fun it was to be flying again. But, as we all know, what goes up, must come

K-Thud!

down. And, according to Bully Boy, what comes down must

"AUGH . . ."

go up again.

And so our little game continued:

"AUGH . . ." *K-Thud!*
"AUGH . . ." *K-Thud!*
"AUGH . . ." *K-Thud!*

But after a while, even that got boring. I mean, when you've experienced one compound fracture, you've experienced them all. By the looks of things, my new playmate must have thought so, too. So, for his grand finale, he stuck his horns even farther inside (nearly making me the world's first human shish kebab), lifted Barrel Buddy and me high over his head, then rolled his neck around and around, which meant we went around and around . . . until, suddenly, with all of his might, he threw back his head, and we shot up faster than a greased space shuttle—almost as high, too. Which, of course, enabled me to continue perfecting my fine art of

"AUGHHHHH"ing

In fact, he tossed us so hard that we flew over his fence and onto the dirt road outside the pen. Now we were back to our simple

*roll, roll, roll*ing . . .

routine. That was great, no sweat. Well, except for the

HONK . . . HONK, HONK, HONK!

livestock truck coming straight at us. *LIVE-STOCK TRUCK COMING STRAIGHT AT US?!*
I'm afraid so.

Now, I don't know the last time you've been inside a rolling barrel, but these things are not as easy to steer as you might think.

HONK . . . HONK, HONK, HONK!

Unless, of course, you get the newer models that come complete with power windows, CD player, and—oh yeah—a steering wheel. But this was obviously an older version that

HONK . . . HONK, HONK, HONK!

had none of those luxuries . . . which meant the only way to avoid becoming livestock-truck road kill was to crawl out of my little spinning barrel of death and—

HONK . . . HONK, HONK, HONK!

All right. I hear you already!

So, some way, somehow I inched myself to the very edge of the barrel. This allowed me to do two things:

1. See the truck's giant tire (complete, of course, with the giant truck) less than six feet from my face. And to

2. Leap out of the barrel for my life.

So after saying a fond farewell to Barrel Buddy and promising to write, I leaped. Basically, it was a pretty good leap. Well, except for the part of my

bounce . . . bounce . . .
"OUCH, OUCH!"
*. . . skid, skidd*ing *. . .*

down the road (without any of your standard bouncing and skidding protective headgear). Still, I succeeded in veering out of the tire's way (not to mention the truck's). And then with just a few more *bounces, skids,* and *ouches,* I finally and at long last—

K-BAMB!

hit a nice, sturdy tree. A nice sturdy tree that immediately sent me into the land of unconsciousness. But even as I was drifting off, I managed to squeeze out one last thought regarding Chad Diamond:
*Now it was **really** time for revenge!*

Chapter 8

War!

The good news was, when they eventually found my body, I hadn't died, yet.

The bad news was, I hurt so much, I wished I had. I mean, I had bruises from the tip of my hair to the end of my toenails . . . and everywhere in between. But Parents' Day was tomorrow, and I had to hurry up and recover, because tomorrow was my last day to make sure Chad Diamond experienced my full wrath.

Cowboy Roy told me to take the rest of the day off and get some rest. I was really touched by his care and compassion—especially the part where he tenderly explained, "I don't care if ya die two days from now, but tomorrow I need a clown."

I'd sent out word for Wall Street to come visit me. I had to tell her what I'd learned about Chad and his little plan. But she told Opera she wasn't interested in what I had to say. She said she was still real mad at me and hadn't forgiven me. To be honest, as much as Satan Breath had hurt me, those words hurt even more. After all, weren't we supposed to be best friends (even if she is a girl)? Still, if that's the way she wanted it, then that's the way she'd have it.

A couple hours earlier Opera and I had worked out a plan on how to get even with Chad. I don't want to brag, but I gotta tell you it was going to be a doozie. Now it was just a matter of waiting until tomorrow. And what fun is waiting without doing a little writing on my superhero story. So, grabbing Ol' Betsy, I went to work:

When we last left Chester C. Chessclub he was zooming across the country in his Nerd-Mobile to Carl's-*REALLY*-Bad Cavern. For it is here that the notorious, not-so-nice nut case, 2-Kool 4 U, is transforming the world's water so that all who drink it will become hyperly hip.

Thanks to his latest supernerd computer, along with his supergeeky calculations, our hero knows he has just arrived outside the hideout. (The fact that his ears are bleeding from all the pounding rap music is a pretty good clue, too.)

So, in a flash of superclumsiness, he stumbles from his Nerd-Mobile (a 1962 Nash Rambler for any adults who are interested), pushes up his taped-up glasses, and rearranges the pencils in his pocket protector.

Now, finally, he's ready to face his felonious foe.

He steps into the mouth of the dark cave and shouts, "2-Kool, are you in here ... here ... here? Hello ... hello ... hello? Echo ... echo ... echo?"

And then, suddenly, directly behind him our hero hears ...

"Well, take a lookie here,
the chump's finally done made it.
Out tryin' to save the world,
when he's got less than a minute."

Chester C. spins around and, sure enough, it's 2-Kool. (If you can't tell by the lousy rhymes, you can tell by the shaved head, sunglasses, and the body piercing—the dude has more rivets in his body than a naval shipyard.)

"2-Kool!" Chester C. shouts over
the pounding music. "You must stop
this craziness!"

"I done gave ya a minute,
to be doin' your thing.
Now it's 53 seconds,
'fore my coolness reigns supreme."

"Fifty-three seconds!" our hero
shouts.

"I said 53 seconds
to do what you gotta do.
But now it's 45,
'fore I make this ol' world too——"

"All right! All right!" our hero
shouts. "I get the idea!"
But, try as he might, he can't think
of anything to do. The clock is ticking
down with just seconds left to save the
world, but nothing comes to mind. No
plan, no words, no nothing. . . .

I stared at the screen, trying to think of something, anything, but the ideas just wouldn't come.

What was going on? Normally these stories take off by themselves, and it's all my little pinkies can do to keep up with them on the keyboard. But now there was nothing, as in zilch, as in nada, as in zippo.

But I already knew the reason. It had nothing to do with the story or even my imagination. Instead, it had everything to do with my wanting revenge. Because, no matter how hard I tried to think about something else, my mind just kept going back to Chad Diamond and getting even. I don't want to say that it had taken over my thinking, but—well, all right, it *had* taken over my thinking. Completely. No matter what I did, it just kept growing and growing and growing some more. Even as I shut down Ol' Betsy and tried to go to sleep, getting even was all I could think about. Because if everything went according to my plan, I'd be getting even in a very, very big way.

Unfortunately, we all know about my plans . . .

* * * * *

Parents' Day started out normal enough. By midmorning we'd suited up in our different costumes and greeted our folks as they rolled into the parking lot. Of course, my parents responded exactly like I knew they would. . . .

"Oh, Wally, you look so adorable." (That, of course, would be Mom.)

"A wimp??! They got my boy dressed up and wearing makeup like a girl??!!" (That, of course, would be Dad.) "I sent you here to become a man, not some sort of, of, of . . ."

"Clown," Mom said helpfully. "He's dressed up as a clown, sweetheart. And a very cute one at that."

> *Honk-a Honk-a*
> (That, of course, would be
> her squeezing my red-ball nose.)
> (Thanks, Mom.)

Speaking of red, I don't think I ever saw Dad turn so many different shades of it. I could tell the poor guy was about to blow a head gasket, so I quickly directed them toward the grandstands where they could get a good seat to watch the show. After a little more fussing and fuming from Dad (and one more *Honk-a Honk-a* from Mom), they finally headed for their seats.

It was then I spotted Wall Street with her mom. I headed on over to greet them.

"Oh, Wally," her mom said, "you look so, so—"

"Yeah, I know," I said, "adorable."

"Actually, I was going to say 'wimpy.'" She grinned, having obviously heard my dad.

"Thanks." I grinned back.

"Seriously," she turned to Wall Street, "doesn't he look cute?"

"Whatever," Wall Street mumbled, not even looking at me.

Her mom threw me a glance. It was obvious she sensed something was wrong, but before she had a chance to say anything, Wall Street suddenly lit up like a Christmas tree. "There he is. There he is!" Taking her mom by the hand she practically dragged her toward Chad, who was approaching with someone who looked like his chauffeur.

"Chad, this is my mom. Mom, this is Chad Diamond."

"Pleased to meet you," Wall Street's mom said. "I've heard so much about you."

Chad looked up from speaking with his chauffeur. "I'm terribly sorry," he said. "Who?"

"I'm Wall Street's mother," she said. "My daughter has spoken so much about you."

Chad's face broke into a quizzical frown. "Excuse me . . ."

"This is my mom," Wall Street said.

The frown deepened. "I see. And who exactly are you?"

For a moment Wall Street stared. Then she broke into nervous laughter. "Oh, I get it. Very funny. Ha-ha. Anyway, I wanted to—"

"I see nothing funny about it, miss," Chad said in his snootiest voice. "Now, if you'll excuse me, we have business to attend to." With that he turned and started to walk off.

Wall Street just stood there, staring . . . until she heard the laughter of some of Chad's nearby buddies. She turned to see them all standing there, listening. Doing her best to ignore them, she ran after him. "Chad . . . Chad."

She caught his arm, and he turned back.

He was obviously put out. "What is it now?"

"I thought we were . . . you know . . . friends."

"Me? Friends? With the likes of you?" He gave a smirking laugh. "I hardly think that's possible." Then, shaking her off, he turned and walked away.

I was wrong about Dad's face turning the hottest red ever. By the looks of things, Wall Street's face was five million degrees hotter. And the laughter of Chad's nearby goons didn't help, either. Yes sir, she had been embarrassed in a very big and very mean way.

But that was okay, because Chad was about to get his in an even bigger and meaner way. Revenge, here we come. . . .

* * * * *

Forty-five minutes later everyone's parents were sitting up in the grandstands above the arena waiting for the show to begin. There was no fence separating the seats from the arena so everyone felt nice and close. As I said before, we all had our assignments. Some got to be rodeo stars, while Opera got to be the concession cart pusher and I was a goofy clown. But that was okay, because Opera and I had a little extracurricular entertainment planned. . . .

"You all set?" I called to him as we met at the horse pen.

He nodded. With one hand he was pouring a bag of chips into his mouth (pre-drenched, of course, with Pecos Bill's Flame Thrower Hot Sauce). With the other he was holding a bucket that Chad's horse was eating out of.

"Did you get the coffee?" I shouted over his Walkman.

He shook his head and yelled, "Coffee maker is busted."

Disappointment started to wash over me. The plan was already failing before it began. "So what's in the bucket?" I asked.

He looked up and grinned. "Coffee beans. Fifteen pounds of prime-roasted coffee beans."

My disappointment turned to anticipation. "That's going to be even better."

He nodded and continued feeding the horse.

"Hey, Wally."

I looked up to see Wall Street joining us. "Hey," I said. Then, after a century or two of uneasiness, I added, "I'm really sorry 'bout that thing with Chad."

She shrugged. "He's a jerk. I should have listened to you."

More silence. Well, except for Chad's horse munching and crunching. I tell you, that animal was really wolfing down those coffee beans.

"So what are you guys doing back here with the horses?" she asked.

I grinned. "Payback time."

Opera nodded and shouted, "Big payback time."

"For Chad?"

"Who else?"

It was Wall Street's turn to grin. "So what can I do to help?"

I grinned back. "Thought you'd never ask."

* * * * *

Ten minutes later and the show was in full swing. Chad had mounted his horse and eased

him into the box. The caffeine from all that coffee had really made the animal jumpy. He was
prancing and dancing like there were burs
under his saddle. In fact, it was all Chad could
do to stay on him. "Whoa, boy!" he kept shouting. "Easy now! Easy now!"

The three of us exchanged knowing smiles.
But the fun and games had barely begun. . . .

"Stand by," Cowboy Roy shouted to Chad.

Chad nodded and threw a glance over to the
chute where the calf was ready to be released.
The calf he was supposed to chase down and rope.

Now it was time to begin Part Two of our
little plan. . . .

"Oh, Chad," I cried, holding up a camera to
take his picture. He saw me and, thanks to his
huge ego, couldn't resist the opportunity to pose
and smile. I fired off a picture, or two, or three

FLASH! FLASH! FLASH!

and was immediately followed by Wall Street
shouting, "Over here, Chad!"

Though my flashes had partially blinded
him, he couldn't resist looking over to Wall
Street and again posing for

FLASH! FLASH! FLASH! FLASH!

four more photos.

"Oh, Chad," I shouted.

Again he looked, and again:

FLASH! FLASH! FLASH! FLASH!

By now the poor guy was so blind he couldn't see a thing. But we still weren't finished. I gave Opera the signal, and he reached through the fence to offer Chad's horse a little drink—you know, something to help wash down all those coffee beans. But instead of water, it was an entire jar of, you guessed it, Pecos Bill's Flame Thrower Hot Sauce.

After two, three, four gulps, the horse suddenly reared up. Then he took off out of the box like a rocket, his mouth blazing with fire. And Chad, poor Chad, it was all he could do just to hang on.

They say revenge isn't supposed to be sweet, but I've got to tell you it was the funniest thing I ever saw . . . blind Chad, unable to see where he's going, bouncing on an out-of-control horse that was running, jumping, and bucking crazily around the ring, desperately searching for something to put out the fire in its mouth.

It was great. And greater still was the way the entire grandstands roared with laughter. I mean,

the guy was definitely dying of embarrassment—
just the way we wanted it—while Wall Street,
Opera, and I were dying with laughter.

Well, we were dying with laughter . . . until
the horse finally found some water to put out its
fire. Unfortunately, that water wasn't in the
arena, it was in a trough in the corral next to
the arena. The corral that belonged to . . . Satan
Breath. The corral whose fence Chad's horse
suddenly

K-RASH!

busted through.

Immediately, Satan Breath charged out, puffing and snorting like a steam engine gone
berserk. Once in the arena, he stopped and glared
about, obviously not in one of his better moods.
And then he saw them . . . all those nice people up
in the stands. All those nice people with no fence
between them and him. All those nice people who
would make wonderful human dartboards.

The big animal lowered his head.

"BROOOO . . ."

Then he began snorting and pawing the earth.
From past experience, I knew what was coming

next. But the audience didn't. Instead, they grew strangely quiet—but only for a moment.

Because in the next moment, Satan Breath charged.

And all those nice people? They were suddenly running and screaming for their lives!

Chapter 9

Somebody . . . *Anybody?* . . . to the Rescue!

After a dozen tries, the crazed bull finally managed to lunge into the stands. He definitely had one thought on his mind. So did the people. They ran and jumped and scattered like rats from a sinking ship. Like lemmings off a cliff. Like people running, jumping, and scattering from one very angry bull. The big fellow had a point to make with those sharp horns, but nobody felt like sticking around to let him make it.

I looked desperately about until I spotted Cowboy Roy standing by the calf chute. He was frozen in fear. I began running toward him. "Cowboy Roy!"

Flip-flop . . . fall

"Cowboy Roy!"

Flip-flop . . . fall

When I finally arrived, I shouted, "You've got to stop him! You've got to do something!"

But he just stood there staring as if he hadn't heard.

"COWBOY ROY!?"

"Huh . . ." He looked at me from someplace far, far away.

"You've got to get Satan Breath back into his pen! You've got to save those people!"

But he just kept standing there. I could tell he was desperate to help, but he was too scared to move.

I turned back to the stands. Fortunately, the people were a lot better at running on the steep steps than the bull. (And a lot better at leaping off them to the ground.) The good news was, Satan Breath hadn't been able to hurt a single one of them. The bad news was, that made him all the more angry. In frustration, he finally turned and half-stumbled, half-fell down the steps until he was back in the arena.

Good. Now at least everyone was safe. Well, almost everyone . . .

He turned his big head from side to side, huffing and puffing and snorting. And then he stopped. Something had caught his eye.

Something over in his corral. I turned to look.

I wished I hadn't.

'Cause there, at the bull's watering trough, stood Chad's horse. He was gulping down the water like there was no tomorrow. But Chad was no longer on him. Instead, he lay on the ground a dozen yards away, flat on his back. It looked like he'd been thrown off, and it looked like he wasn't planning on getting up for a while.

Satan Breath gave a loud snort. Then he began pawing the earth. Finally, he lowered his head.

I spun to Cowboy Roy. "You've got to do something!" I shouted. "He's going to get Chad!!"

But Cowboy Roy just kept staring. Oh, he tried to answer. He even managed to open his mouth. But the words would not come. It was exactly like Mrs. Cowboy Roy had said—he was scared to death of bulls and nothing could change it. Not even some kid about to get killed.

Desperately, I looked all around the arena, then up to the stands. There was no one to help. No one but Cowboy Roy.

"You've got to do something!!" I shouted. "You've got to help him!" But the poor guy just stood there, doing nothing.

I spun back to Satan Breath. He was still snorting and pawing . . . building up his power . . . and his hatred. Any second he would charge.

Chad lay on the ground less than thirty feet from the big animal. Somebody had to do something! And since I was the only somebody around, I guess that somebody had to be me. (Don't you just hate it when that happens?) Before anyone could shout to stop me (and believe me, I was listening real hard for anybody), I took a deep breath, said a quick prayer, and

> *Flip-flop . . . fall*
> *Flip-flop . . . fall*

raced into the arena.

"Wally, what are you doing?!" Opera yelled.

"Wally!!" Wall Street screamed.

But I'd already made up my mind. I raced toward the monstrous creature shouting, "Hey! Hey, you! Hey, Satan Breath!"

Unfortunately, the animal heard. With a loud, angry snort, he spun his head around to me.

"Yeah," I shouted, "I'm talking to you!"

And then, as if I hadn't done enough damage, I happened to remember what Mrs. Cowboy Roy had said about my little spinning bow tie. *"That's what Roy used to use to attract the bulls in the rodeo."*

Oh, great, I thought, *just great. Now for sure I'm going to get myself killed.*

Reluctantly, I reached into my baggy pants pocket. My hands were shaking so hard, it took a moment to find the little button. Unfortunately, I found it. Unfortunatelier, I gave it a squeeze.

Immediately, the little red bow tie lit up and started to spin.

And immediately I had Satan Breath's undivided attention.

Any confusion he had about whether to attack Chad or me was definitely cleared up now. The big animal snorted angrily, then whirled his entire body around to face me.

So there I stood, trying to remember how to swallow.

So there he stood, pawing the ground, preparing to charge.

I lowered my head and began to pray.

He lowered his head and . . .

BEGAN RACING TOWARD ME!

Now, the way I figured it, I had two choices . . .

1. I could stand there and immediately get killed,

or

2. I could run for my life and delay the process by about 3.2 seconds.

Decisions, decisions . . .

"BROOOO . . ."

But since I hadn't had much exercise that day
. . . and since running was supposed to be good for
the heart, I decided to run. Run for my life and

"AUGH!"

scream. Well, actually,

Flip-flop . . . fall
Flip-flop . . . fall

for my life and scream. Still, I was luring ol'
Bully Boy away from Chad, and that was the
important thing.

Up ahead, I spotted one of the barrels from
Wall Street's barrel race. And since I'd become
such an expert at barrel riding and since Satan
Breath was less than ten feet away from making
me his personal horn ornament, I

Flip-flop . . . fell

toward it until I arrived and

Flip-flop . . . leaped

inside it.

I tell you, it was great to be back home. Who knows, with a little remodeling, maybe hanging a picture or two, I could really get used to the place. Except, of course, for:

K-thud
roll, roll, roll
K-thud
roll, roll, roll

my pesky neighbor. Thanks to him, everything was again spinning around and around and around some more until, suddenly, my home away from home

K-BAMB!

slammed into a fence post. Lucky for me, we hit so hard that the spinning stopped. Not so lucky for me, we hit so hard that I was

Tumble, Tumble, Tumble

thrown out of the barrel.

So there I was, out in the middle of the arena, counting my broken bones and wondering how many organs I'd need transplanted when I once again heard:

"BROOOO . . ."
snort, snort, snort
paw, paw, paw

I crawled to my hands and knees just in time to see my old pal dropping his head and again preparing to charge. This time, however, I had no protection. This time we were going at it head to head. Not a great idea considering the hardness of his and the softness of mine. Even less of a great idea considering those troublesome horns.

"Run, Wally! Run!" I glanced over my shoulder to see Cowboy Roy. It was good to know he'd finally found his voice. But by the looks of things, he still hadn't found his courage. His expression said he was majorly worried and majorly concerned. (Probably 'cause I'd soon be majorly dead.)

"Run!" He kept shouting. "Get on your feet and run!"

I would have obeyed, but with my recent barrel spinning routine, I was so dizzy I couldn't find my feet . . . let alone the ground to put them on.

"Run, Wally! Run!"

But it was no good. I was too dizzy. I tried but couldn't stand. I looked back to Cowboy Roy. The man was a picture of panic. "Run!" he shouted. "RUN! RUN!"

Again I tried and again I fell. There was nothing I could do. There was, however, something Satan Breath could do . . .

He let out one final snort, pawed the earth . . . and charged!

"WALLY!"

I could hear the big animal snorting and puffing. I could feel the ground shaking and trembling. I could feel my heart stopping.

"WALLY!"

I looked over to Cowboy Roy one last time. And to my surprise, an amazing thing was happening. Something inside him had snapped. It was like he was going crazy. All at once, he was leaping over the fence and racing into the arena. He ran straight toward us, waving his hands and yelling. It was a thrilling sight . . . and one I was more than a little grateful to see.

However, I would have been a bit more grateful, if it had been, oh, maybe two or three minutes earlier. Because at that exact moment I noticed a pair of bull horns driving toward my chest. A pair of bull horns attached to one very large bull. In a desperate attempt to avoid open-heart surgery, I rolled to one side . . . and just in time. The good news was, his horns missed my body.

The bad news was, they didn't miss my suspenders.

Somehow he got his horns hung up in them, which was okay, until he lifted up his head. Because by lifting up his head, he also lifted up me. Even that was okay except for the . . .

B-oing . . .
B-oing . . . B-oing . . .

That's right. Suddenly, I was bouncing up and down in front of the big animal's face like a human yo-yo. And each *b-oing* dropped me right in front of those hateful eyes and that snorting snout.

B-oing . . . SNORT
B-oing . . . SNORT
B-oing . . . SNORT

"Drop him!" Cowboy Roy shouted as he raced toward us. "Drop him!"

Now, to be honest, I didn't know if being dropped directly in front of Satan Breath was such a good idea or not—considering all those hoofs and horns and everything. But it didn't matter. Ol' Bully Boy had other ideas. Instead of dropping me, he began swinging his head back and forth, then around and around, anything to get me unstuck. Suddenly, I was doing a lot less *B-oing*ing and a lot more

"WOAAA . . . WHAAA . . . WEEEE . . ."

twirling. Around and around I went, faster and faster, until finally

K-TwanG!

the suspenders gave way, and I took off like a giant slingshot.

The good news was, I was finally free of Satan Breath. The better news was, I was sailing high over his fence. The bad news was, on the other side of the fence was my ol' buddy, the giant cowpie!

For the most part, it was a pleasant flight, though I wish they'd have included a meal or an in-flight movie. Still, the view was pretty good as I caught a glimpse of Cowboy Roy doing all of his old clown stuff—distracting Satan Breath away from Chad while shouting at Wall Street and Opera to get in there and pull the kid out.

Yes sir, it was a beautiful sight and one I would have enjoyed a bit longer, if it weren't for my

K-PLOP!

face-first landing.

Still, despite the sudden clogging of my eyes, nose, mouth, and ears, it was great to know that Chad Diamond was in good hands. It was great to know he was going to be okay.

Chapter 10

Wrapping Up

When we last left Chester C. Chessclub he had finally come face to face with the sinister 2-Kool 4 U. Unfortunately, the mind of our author was so taken over with thoughts of revenge that he couldn't think of anything to write. But now that his brain is clear (as well as his conscience), he finally puts Chester C. into action. In a flash of superior superheroism, Chester C. Chessclub leaps at the creepily chilly criminal. Basically, it's a pretty good leap, scoring an 8.9 with the Olympic judges—and if it weren't for the tiny matter of stepping on his cape and

K-Stumble

falling flat on his face, he might
have even brought home a medal.

But mere clumsiness is not enough
to stop our beloved hero. Not on your
life (or his). Jumping back to his
feet, he immediately stubs his toe on
a stalactite or a stalagmite (I can
never remember which is which), hits
his head on a stalagmite (or a stalactite), and staggers around so
cluelessly that the radical rapper
finally raps:

"Quit that messin' and a-foolin'
Quit doin' what you're doin'
'Cause this water I'm a brewin's
'Bout ta make our world a cool one."

And then, just when the rhyming
can't get any worse, just when it
looks like there'll never be another
song with a real melody again—

Ta-Daaa!

Oh, no . . .

"What's that?" 2-Kool cries.
"What's happenin'?!"

"It's me. (*Da-da . . . taaaaa*) Music Guy."

"And me. (*K-Bang, K-Pow*) Sound Effects Guy."

"Listen," the author types, "I'm
just about done writing this story,
can't you wait until—"

"But you promised me and
Sound Effects Guy that we would talk."

"That's right, and (*K-Boink, K-Bop*) by
the look of the few pages you have left, we're
almost out of (*K-Blewy!*) room."

"Hey, man," 2-Kool asks, "who are
these fools?"

"We help the author tell his
(*Dee-dee-dum*) story."

"Well, now," 2-Kool says, "that's
kinda cool."

"And speaking of cool (*K-Bamb*), we're

here to tell you that you're not nearly
as cool as you think you are."

**Suddenly, 2-Kool's face clouds into
an un-cool frown. "What you be sayin'?"**

"I'm saying that the real cool people (*K-Bing*)
don't go around trying to look cool or sound
cool."

"He's (*Ta-Taaa*) right!"

"Uh, guys . . ." the author types.

"Not now."

"But . . ."

"We'll (*K-plop*) take it from here."

"You see, cool is (*Ta-da Daaaa*) just
being who you are. It's not trying to be
something or someone else.
It's just being . . . you."

"That's (*B-oing, B-oing*) right. You can be a
sound effects guy—"

"Or a (*Da-da Taaaa*) music guy—"

"Or a superhero?" Chester C. chimes in.

"Or a superhero. The point is (*K-bamb,
tinkle, tinkle, tinkle*), cool is being who
God made you to be and becoming what
He wants you to become."

"You mean I don't have to be a-talkin'
Or try to be a-shockin'
With these fancy rhymes of mine
All the time?"

"Only if you (*K-smack*) want to."

"Also (*Ta-taaaa*) it's cooler not to force
people to fit into *your* version of cool. Let
them be cool how they want to be cool."

"Well, now, hmmm. That *is* kinda cool."

"Exact(*K-Boink*)ly."

"Go ahead," 2-Kool says, "be tellin'
me some more 'bout this cooler way to
be cool."

"You (*K-Burp*) bet!"

And so the three continue talking—
2-Kool, Sound Effects Guy, and Music
Guy——as they stroll out of the cave
and toward the setting sun, knowing
that the world is a safer and better
place to——
"Hey," Chester C. calls after them,
"what about me?"

"I guess you and the author are going to have
to dream up another (*Dum-de-dum*)
story with a different bad guy."

"That's right," 2-Kool calls back,
"'cause I ain't gonna be bad no more.
I'm just gonna be ... cooool."
And so we come to another sappy and
somewhat silly ending——
"Let alone stupid," Chester C.
mutters.
"What do you mean?" the author types.
"I mean, isn't the hero supposed to
be the one who gets to save the day
and not a bunch of music and sound
effects guys?"

"Well, yes, that's true, but I was going for something a little different here."

"So what am I supposed to do now?"

"Why don't you let me finish this last paragraph and then maybe——"

"Hey, I got a better idea," Chester C. says. "Why don't we go to Wal-Mart and look at all the new pocket protectors?"

"Well, I don't——"

"Or how 'bout those neato-keen chessboards they got in?"

"Um ..."

"Better yet, I hear they got a brand-new shipment of laptop computers. Maybe the two of us could——"

"Laptop computers!" the author types. "What are we waiting for! Let's get going!"

And so, as the sun sinks slowly into the West, our hero and his author race to the nearest Wal-Mart with the assurance that the world is once again a safer, saner, and yes, even cooler place to live, now that everybody can be themselves.

"Hey, Wally, *munch, munch,* your folks are out(*burp*)side waiting to go."

I glanced up to see Opera standing at the door to our bunkhouse. I nodded, hit "Save," and quickly packed Ol' Betsy away. Once outside I saw all the campers were busy loading into their cars, saying their good-byes, and promising to write.

"Hey, McDoogle." I turned to see Chad Diamond. He was already in the backseat of his limo getting ready to go. "What you did in that arena for me . . ." He cleared his throat, and I could tell it was pretty hard for him to continue. "It was, uh, well, it was pretty cool."

I shrugged. "I figured it was the least I could do, considering what I did." Then, lowering my voice a little, I added, "I really want to apologize for that. Even though Wall Street and I are best friends, that's no excuse."

It was his turn to shrug. "Forget it, I did the same thing to you, only worse." Then with a grin he added, "Maybe we'll do it again next year."

I shook my head. "No, I learned my lesson, Chad. It doesn't matter what you do to me, I'm not going to try to get even."

He looked at me kinda funny. "Really?" he said. "That's kinda lame."

"Actually, seeking revenge is what's lame."

"Besides . . ." We both turned to see Mrs. Cowboy Roy approaching the limo. "It don't look like there'll be a next year."

My heart sank. "We messed things up that bad for you?" I asked.

"No"—she shook her head—"just the opposite. Remember how I was a-sayin' that Roy Boy and me was only running a kiddies' ranch to help meet expenses? You know, so the bank wouldn't shut us down?"

"Yeah."

"It seems yer little prank helped my husband get his courage back." She spat in her cup. "For the first time in years he's back to his old self. Now there's a good chance we can get the ranch up on its feet without havin' to put up with all you kids."

I broke into a grin. "That's great."

"We sure think so." She tousled my hair. "'Course, Roy would never say it to you in person, so I'll have to say it for him."

"Say what?"

It was her time to grin. "Thanks, Wally."

I nodded and looked up just in time to see Dad pulling the van beside us. "All right," he called, "let's get going, Son."

My mouth dropped open. "Son"? Had he actually

called me "Son"? I couldn't believe it. I mean,
usually it's "Hey you," or on a real good day,
"Wallace, you moron!!!" But, "Son"? For a minute
it almost sounded like he was happy we were
related. And by the smile creeping around the
corners of his mouth, I almost figured he was.

After saying my good-byes and promising to
write, I finally climbed into the van.

"Good news," Dad said as we started to pull
away. "Since you did so well here, I've found a
bunch of great camp ideas for next year."

"No kidding?" I croaked.

"Yes, sir," he said. "Now that you've proven
yourself a real man, there's all sorts of camps we
can choose from. For starters, what do you think
of the World HeavyWeight Wrestling Camp?"

I tried not to groan. "Not bad," I said, "if you
don't mind me being crushed by some hairy
gorilla."

"Actually, that's another camp," he said. "The
Baboon Training School in Africa."

"The what?!"

"Sure. Then there's that Snake Handling
Camp in South America, or the Alligator
Wrestling Camp in Florida, or the Skydiving
School in Arizona, or the Lumberjack Camp, or
Hang Gliding, or Bungee Jumping, or . . ."

Dad continued rattling off one method of

dying after another. I didn't want to ruin his fun by explaining that the only way I could go to another summer camp was if I somehow survived another school year. (And, as we all know, the chances of that are pretty slim.) Instead, I glanced out the window to see Mr. and Mrs. Cowboy Roy, waving to the kids and spitting in perfect unison.

And still Dad kept going down his list: "Then there's S.W.A.T. Camp, or the Bomb Squad Camp, or Nuclear Reactor Camp . . ."

Yes sir, somehow I expected that the fun and games weren't entirely over; that my incredible worlds would just keep on getting more incredible.

"Or the Vampire Trapping Camp in Transylvania, or the Guided Missile Camp in Russia . . ."

Anyway, I'll see you again next time . . .

"Or the Polar Bear Feeding Camp in Alaska . . ."

. . . if I'm lucky.